THE YOUNG VISITERS

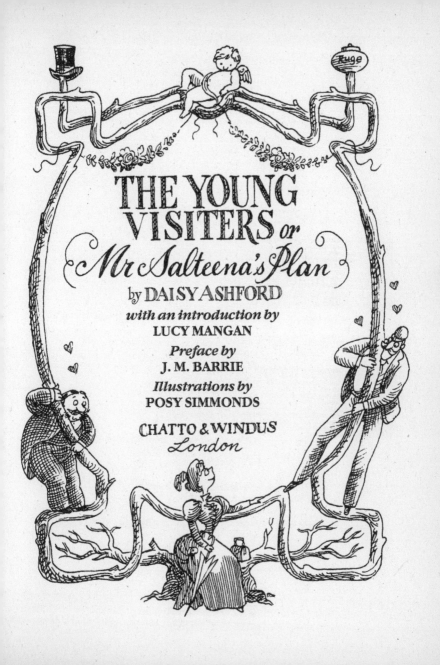

THE YOUNG VISITERS *or*
Mr Salteena's Plan

by DAISY ASHFORD

with an introduction by
LUCY MANGAN

Preface by
J. M. BARRIE

Illustrations by
POSY SIMMONDS

CHATTO & WINDUS
London

1 3 5 7 9 10 8 6 4 2

Chatto & Windus, an imprint of Vintage,
20 Vauxhall Bridge Road,
London SW1V 2SA

Chatto & Windus is part of the Penguin Random House group of companies
whose addresses can be found at global.penguinrandomhouse.com.

Penguin
Random House
UK

First published by Chatto & Windus in 1919
19th impression 1936
First issued in the Zodiac Books in an illustrated edition 1949
Reprinted 1950
New edition 1951
13th impression 1983
First published in a Folio Society edition 1956
New edition 1984
This edition 2019

penguin.co.uk/vintage

A CIP catalogue record for this book is available from the British Library

ISBN 9781784743215

Typeset in 11/14.2 pt Garamond
by Integra Software Services Pvt. Ltd, Pondicherry

Printed and bound in Great Britain by Clays Ltd, Elcograf S.p.A.

Penguin Random House is committed to a sustainable future
for our business, our readers and our planet. This book is
made from Forest Stewardship Council® certified paper.

CONTENTS

INTRODUCTION

EVERYTHING about *The Young Visiters* is a joy. The story of the child who wrote it and the woman she grew up to be, the story of how it came to be published – and, of course, the story of Mr Salteena and Ethel Monticue itself. There is a charm and a purity to it all that is redolent of a vanished age. I first read the tale in my twenties and had the odd experience, not repeated with any book I have come across in a long and varied reading career, of laughing myself sick even as I felt my soul being cleansed. The combination of innocence and acuity quite undid me.

The author, Daisy Ashford, was famously only nine years old when she produced her enduring masterpiece in 1890. 'I really cannot remember what started me on writing,' she wrote much later to her publisher. 'Unless it came from a love of reading, for I remember as a very small child reading aloud to one of my step-brothers – a novel – and this possibly gave me the idea of writing one myself.'

Daisy's mother Emma was a widow with five children when she was introduced by her parish priest to fellow Catholic William Ashford, a bachelor at forty-three. They married in 1880 and Daisy was born a year later. Two sisters, Vera then Angie, followed. It was a happy 'blended family', as we would now say, with a slightly bohemian, unorthodox approach to family life that benefitted the younger members in particular. Emma was a lively wit who would whisk the children out of lessons and off for picnics on a whim. She once wrote and produced a very successful local pantomime in rhyme, and after holding a fancy-dress ball sent every guest a printed booklet of limericks she had written about all of them. William was a calmer, more serious presence but still not the stereotypical strict Victorian patriarch. Daisy, Vera and Angie often went unchaperoned, were all educated at home and encouraged to roam his library at will, allowing Daisy exposure to all sorts of novels, forms, tones and literary voices whose influence we can see filtered through her nine-year-old consciousness in *The Young Visiters*. The family were also comfortably off, with servants and plenty of guests and callers at the house to provide real-life grist to a latent novelist's mill.

Despite Daisy's tender age, *The Young Visiters* was not her first composition. In testimony both to her precocity and, I believe, the patience of her parents, she had already served a long apprenticeship. From at least the age of three she was dictating long letters to her beloved aunt, Julia. One, taken down in Emma's hand, ends 'With Papa's best love & his head & his towdowders I remain a good woman. You're a good woman and Father's a good gekleum'.

I feel it only fair to note that even at this early stage, her parents were instinctively aware of the importance of preserving childish pronunciations and spellings for comedy value.

A year later, in 1885, a Jesuit priest came to stay with the family, with whom Daisy became fascinated. She told William that she wanted to write his Life, whereupon her father pulled out a pen and paper and suggested she begin right away. She did, pacing up and down the room with her hands behind her back, dictating to William the first instalment of what would become (recorded in both parents' writing, so presumably over several sessions) a 4,000-word biography – entirely invented – called 'The Life of Father McSwiney'. Reading it now, her talent – if as yet relatively untrammelled by craft – is clear. The Life is fresh, lively and fast-flowing, as well as full of inadvertent moments for laughter (I particularly admire the Pope's call for mashed potatoes and gravy in the middle of supper). Its length and resolution also speak to something perhaps even rarer than storytelling ability in a child – application, without which *The Young Visiters* would surely not be half as strikingly structured or eminently readable as it is.

A story called 'Mr Chapmer's Bride' (now lost) followed, and then 'A Short Story of Love and Marriage' (those noble subjects covered in the first chapter and the second and final chapter respectively) when she was eight. Daisy's daughter recalled in later life that her mother remembered being admonished by William during one of her dictations for reworking a plot of a book someone had recently read to her. He told her that if she was going to write, it must be her own work – a lesson, says her daughter, Daisy never forgot.

The Young Viseters (as it was originally titled – that spelling was the only one revised before it was released to a wider audience, perhaps because that first extra 'e' puts it just on the wrong side of immediate comprehension for an audience unaware of its origins and the need to read it half through a child's eyes) was the first story she wrote by herself. She did so in a red-covered tuppenny exercise book, with quite serious intent she said much later, though the result has had readers in stitches ever since it was published nearly thirty years after being put away in a drawer with many of Daisy's and her sisters' other creations and forgotten about amid the tumult of daily family life.

It's impossible not to imagine how differently things could have gone now. Would any middle-class parent be content to let their precocious darling simply have fun, keep for private amusement and pleasure what was even in that lively and verbally dextrous family surely a remarkable output, and simply let whatever talent their daughter possessed develop at its own pace? Would there not have been an irresistible humblebrag or two under excerpts on Facebook that did the rounds and eventually got spotted by an eagle-eyed scout for the next till-side Christmas book? Imagine a viral Daisy Ashford. The spirit quails.

But – stand firm! For we are now in 1917. This was the year Emma died and the melancholy task of going through the household's papers and possessions, familiar to anyone who has lost a parent, had to be undertaken. The exercise book was found in a box of their mother's personal mementoes and, despite their grief, rereading *The Young Visiters* gave the sisters much entertainment. So much so, that when Daisy's friend Margaret McKenzie was convalescing from a bout of flu, Daisy gave it to her in the hope that it might cheer her up. Margaret – her sense of humour evidently not dulled by illness – was enchanted. She was a well-connected woman and bruited its charms to many – including to a group of friends during a country weekend. After hearing the first two chapters read aloud, one of them – Frank Swinnerton, a novelist himself and also a reader for the publisher Chatto & Windus – asked if he could read the rest of it in bed that night. He came down the next morning full of the desire to see it in print. Margaret cabled Daisy, got her delighted permission, and Chatto were soon infected with Swinnerton's enthusiasm. They were keen to publish, once they had solved the problem of how to present a work that fell so far outside the norm. In the end, they decided to keep the idiosyncratic spelling intact (save the partially corrected title) but to break up the chapters, which each ran as one long chunk of text, into more traditional paragraphs, for greater ease of readerly passage. And they thought a preface both to explain and assure readers that 'it is the authentic work of a young person', rather than a joke or adult pastiche of some kind, would be necessary.

Swinnerton approached J. M. Barrie, the author of *Peter Pan*, who had become in the wake of its success regarded almost as the custodian of the nation's collective childhood and imagination, to write it. Barrie was enchanted by *The Young Visiters* but advised that it be printed privately or as a magazine article with a running commentary alongside – which is why publishers tend not to pay too much attention to writers when it comes to commercial or marketing decisions. Swinnerton, unmoved from his conviction that the book would work as exactly that and find a ready audience, went to visit the writer. At the end of their meeting, at which Barrie proposed many alternative authors for the job and each one was rejected, a long silence fell. Barrie eventually broke it by saying, 'I see I've got to write this preface.' And he did. It has appeared in every edition of *The Young Visiters*, including this one, ever since Chatto published it in 1919.

All of Swinnerton's instincts were correct. *The Young Visiters* found the readiest of markets and it was reprinting even before it had been published. Within a week of publication, the second printing had sold before the presses had completed their hurried work, along with half of the third and with a fourth duly being lined up. It was an instant bestseller and it garnered almost unanimously ecstatic reviews. 'I never thought in my life,' wrote Daisy to Swinnerton, 'I should experience such a thrill as getting a book published. It really does quite stagger me.'

The only two tiny flies in the ointment were that Daisy hated being interviewed and soon declined to do any, and that rumours – perhaps inevitably – emerged that the preface was a misdirection and Barrie had written the whole thing himself. Such are the perils of fame. One fascinating letter to a periodical as the 'hoax' debate raged ran thus:

We have known many children as intimately as it is ever possible to know them at all, and some of them have been horrid. But we have never known a child horrid enough to write The Young Visiters. As the playful fantasy of an elder, it is charming. As the work of a child, it would be repulsive and contrary to all we have learned to like and admire in our young friends. Children are never facetious; they do not understand snobbery.

Before we return to the many issues raised by this heartfelt missive, let us just note that Chatto & Windus eventually put an end to the matter by producing the original exercise book and by publishing other works by Daisy and her sister Angie. Presumably the additional publicity was no longer worth the unpleasant rumours.

But that letter is interesting in many ways. Partly for the inconsistency of its claim to have known many children and never met one who was facetious or who understood snobbery (what he or she had met, I suspect, is a great number of very polite children who let rip like mini Oscar Wildes as soon as they were safely back in the nursery). But mainly in the way that it seems to have read a completely different book from the one millions of readers have fallen in love with over the last hundred years. For many of us, no doubt, the absolute reverse sentiment to the letter writer's is true; *The Young Visiters* would be unbearable if it had been written as 'a playful fantasy' by an adult. It would be whimsical, twee and altogether revolting.

I think most of us would err instead on the side of the *Manchester Guardian*, whose admiring review said plainly: 'There is nothing fanciful or tender in it.' This is what makes it so striking. It may have been written by a precocious child, but not by one with any consciousness of being so – and therefore without any of the preciousness that so often accompanies that perilous state.

The Young Visiters is hilarious – and the laughter it induces is hearty not wry, and it is bracing not sentimental. Mr Salteena and his compatriots are marched smartly through their plots by an author who knows where she's going and takes the getting there seriously.

To be sure, the inescapable guilelessness and limited life experience of a nine-year-old plays its part. The child's sense of priorities intruding at adult moments – the glory of 'a tip up baison', Mr Salteena bursting into his would-be inamorata Ethel's bedroom to tell her 'excitedly I have had some tea in bed', or Ethel's assurance to new beau Bernard that she will be ready soon 'as I had my bath last night so wont wash very much now' – gladdens even the most calcified heart. The recurrence of ices as the highest possible form of pleasure (though 'countless cakes . . . jelly merangs jam tarts with plenty of jam on each some cold tongue some ham with salid and a pigs head done up in a wondrous manner' should be added for a wedding feast) speaks to us all. And the number of telling details should have scotched the hoaxing rumours as quickly as they began – what adult would remember the importance of ensuring that the tarts had plenty of jam on each? That's a child's recent memory, still carrying the faint tang of betrayal. There is also the simple joy, always, of a child's attempts to emulate grown-up behaviour and conversations overheard and only semi-understood – 'I shall put some red ruuge on my face said Ethel because I am very pale owing to the drains in this house.'

But there is art as well as artlessness in *The Young Visiters*. Daisy wrote with serious intent and, although it is impossible to know the author's heart, I find it almost equally impossible to believe that all her scene-setting descriptions, all her choices, every one of her carefully observed details about her characters are all coincidentally apposite, illustrative and hilarious. This may be an unformed writer at work, but it is unquestionably a writer; selective, active, world-building always with her reader in mind. She knows – by either innate instinct or one so early instilled by her voracious reading as to be indistinguishable from it – how to write her characters with warmth even as she limns and mocks their foibles, when best to leave a scene for another to create suspense and the desire to read on.

Sometimes youth and nascent artistry fuse. All comedies of manners depend on an author being able to view human absurdities with a detached eye. In *The Young Visiters*, the author is detached in a rare way – by her extreme youth – but the perspicacious end is the same: a ruthless parsing of conventions and appreciation of how ridiculous they are, so long uncoupled from whatever purpose they originally served. Or, in the case of Mr Salteena's class-based woes, how flimsy a house of cards it is in which we all live. Not that the author limits herself to his social insecurities. She knows – and nine years of observation is, in this particular case, ample time to become sure of one's facts – that where a fellow admits of one set of doubts there are likely to lurk more. And so we have such moments as our protagonist, when challenged by the 'superier' Procurio to choose the water for his bath, opting for cold, 'feeling it was more manly to say that'. Fragile masculinity, thy name is Salteena.

But in analysing the book's charms we risk becoming the butterfly collector, who kills the thing he loves the better to study it. Let's stop before that happens. The book lies before you, as fresh, charming and funny as ever it was. Curl up and enjoy. A sumpshious repast awaits.

LUCY MANGAN

PREFACE

THE 'owner of the copyright' guarantees that *The Young Visiters* is the unaided effort in fiction of an authoress of nine years. 'Effort', however, is an absurd word to use, as you may see by studying the triumphant countenance of the child herself, which is here reproduced as frontispiece to her sublime work. This is no portrait of a writer who had to burn the oil at midnight (indeed there is documentary evidence that she was hauled off to bed every evening at six): it has an air of careless power; there is a complacency about it that by the severe might perhaps be called smugness. It needed no effort for that face to knock off a masterpiece. It probably represents precisely how she looked when she finished a chapter. When she was actually at work I think the expression was more solemn, with the tongue firmly clenched between the teeth; an unholy rapture showing as she drew near her love chapter. Fellow-craftsmen will see that she is looking forward to this chapter all the time.

The manuscript is in pencil in a stout little note book (twopence), and there it has lain for years, for though the authoress was nine when she wrote it she is now a grown woman. It has lain, in lavender as it were, in the dumpy note book, waiting for a publisher to ride that way and rescue it; and here he is at last, not a bit afraid that to this age it may appear 'Victorian'. Indeed if its pictures of High Life are accurate (as we cannot doubt, the authoress seems always so sure of her facts) they had a way of going on in those times which is really surprising. Even the grand historical figures were free and easy, such as King Edward, of whom we have perhaps the most human picture ever penned, as he appears at a levee 'rarther sumshiously', in a 'small but costly crown', and afterwards slips away to tuck into ices. It would seem in particular that we are oddly wrong in our idea of the young Victorian lady as a person more shy and shrinking than the girl of today. The Ethel of this story is a fascinating creature who would have a good time wherever there were a few males, but no longer could she voyage through life quite so jollily without attracting the attention of the censorious. Chaperon seems to be one of the very few good words of which our authoress had never heard.

The lady she has grown into, the 'owner of the copyright' already referred to, gives us a few particulars of this child she used to be, and is evidently a little scared by her. We should probably all be a little scared (though proud) if that portrait was dumped down in front of us as ours, and we were asked to explain why we once thought so much of ourselves as that.

Except for the smirk on her face, all I can learn of her now is that she was one of a small family who lived in the country, invented their own games, dodged the governess and let the rest of the world go hang. She read everything that came her way, including, as the context amply proves, the grown-up novels of the period. 'I adored writing and used to pray for bad weather, so that I need not go out but could stay in and write.' Her mother used to have early tea in bed; sometimes visitors came to the house, when there was talk of events in high society: there was mention of places called Hampton Court, the Gaiety Theatre and the Crystal Palace. This is almost all that is now remembered, but it was enough for the blazing child. She sucked her thumb for a moment (this is guesswork), and sat down to her amazing tale.

'Her mother used to have early tea in bed.' Many authors must have had a similar experience, but they all missed the possibilities of it until this young woman came along. It thrilled her; and tea in bed at last takes its proper place in fiction. 'Mr Salteena woke up rather early next day and was surprised and delighted to find Horace the footman entering with a cup of tea. Oh thankyou my man said Mr Salteena rolling over in the costly bed. Mr Clarke is nearly out of the bath sir anounced Horace I will have great plesure in turning it on for you if such is your desire. Well yes you might said Mr Salteena seeing it was the idear.' Mr Salteena cleverly conceals his emotion, but as soon as he is alone he rushes to Ethel's door, 'I say said Mr Salteena excitedly I have had some tea in bed.'

'Sometimes visitors came to the house.' Nothing much in that to us, but how consummately this child must have studied them; if you consider what she knew of them; if you consider what she knew of them before the 'viacle' arrived to take them back to the station you will never dare to spend another week-end in a house where there may be a novelist of nine years. I am sure that when you left your bedroom this child stole in, examined everything and summed you up. She was particularly curious about the articles on your dressing-table, including the little box containing a reddish powder, and she never desisted from watching you till she caught you dabbing it on your cheeks. This powder, which she spells 'ruge', went a little to her head, and it accompanies Ethel on her travels with superb effect. For instance, she is careful to put it on to be proposed to; and again its first appearance is excused in words that should henceforth be serviceable in every boudoir: 'I shall put some red ruge on my face said Ethel because I am very pale owing to the drains in this house.'

Those who read will see how the rooms in Hampton Court became the 'compartments' in the Crystal Palace, and how the 'Gaierty' Hotel grew out of the Gaiety Theatre, with many other agreeable changes. The novelist will find the tale a model for his future work. How incomparably, for instance, the authoress dives into her story at once. How cunningly throughout she keeps us on the hooks of suspense, jumping to Mr Salteena when we are in a quiver about Ethel, and turning to Ethel when we are quite uneasy about Mr Salteena. This authoress of nine is flirting with her readers all the time. Her mind is such a rich pocket that as she digs in it (her head to the side and her tongue well out) she sends up showers of nuggets. There seldom probably was a novelist with such an uncanny knowledge of his characters as she has of Mr Salteena. The first line of the tale etches him for all time: 'Mr Salteena was an elderly man of 42 and was fond of asking peaple to stay with him.' On the next page Salteena draws a touching picture of himself in a letter accepting an invitation: 'I do hope I shall enjoy myself with you. I am fond of digging in the garden and I am parshial to ladies

if they are nice I suppose it is my nature. I am not quite a gentleman but you would hardly notice it but cant be helped anyhow.'
'When the great morning came Mr Salteena did not have an egg for
his breakfast in case he should be sick on the jorney.' For my part
I love Mr Salteena, who has a touch of Hamlet, and I wished up
to the end that Ethel would make him happy, though I never had
much hope after I read the descriptions of Bernard Clark's legs.

It is not to be wondered at that Mr Salteena soon grew 'rarther
jellus' of Bernard, who showed off from the first. 'My own room
is next the bath room said Bernard it is decerated dark red as I have
somber tastes. The bath room has got a tip up baison.' Thus was
Mr Salteena put in his place, and there the cruel authoress (with
her tongue farther out than ever) doggedly keeps him. 'After dinner
Ethel played some merry tunes on the piano and Bernard responded with a rather loud song in a base voice and Ethel clapped him
a good deal. Then Mr Salteena asked a few riddles as he was not
musical.' No wonder Mr Salteena went gloomily to bed, not to sleep,
but to think out the greater riddle of how to become a gentleman,
with which triumphant adventure the book is largely concerned.

To many the most instructive part of the story will be the chapter entitled 'Bernards Idear'. Bernard's idear (warmly acclaimed by
Ethel) is that she and he should go up to London 'for a few weeks
Gaierty'. Something of the kind has often been done in fiction and
in guide-books, but never probably in such a hearty way as here.
Arrived at the Gaierty Hotel Bernard pokes his head into the 'window of the pay desk. Have you a coupple of bedrooms for self and
young lady he enquired in a lordly way.' He is told that they have

two beauties. 'Thankyou said Bernard we will go up if you have no objection. None whatever sir said the genial lady the beds are well aired and the view is quite pleasant. Come along Ethel cried Bernard this sounds alright eh. Oh quite said Ethel with a beaming smile.' He decides gallantly that the larger room shall be hers. 'I shall be quite lost in that huge bed,' Ethel says. 'Yes I expect you will said Bernard and now what about a little table d'ote followed by a theater.'

Bernard's proposal should be carried in the pocket of all future swains. He decides 'while imbibing his morning tea beneath his pink silken quilt', that to propose in London would not be the 'correct idear'. He springs out of bed and knocks at Ethel's door. 'Are you up my dear he called. Well not quite said Ethel hastilly jumping from her downy nest.' He explains his idear. 'Oh Hurrah shouted Ethel I shall soon be ready as I had my bath last night so wont wash very much now.'

They go up the river in a boat, and after they had eaten and drunk 'deeply of the charming viands ending up with merangs and choclates', Bernard says 'in a passionate tone' 'Let us now bask under the spreading trees. Oh yes lets said Ethel.' 'Ethel he murmered in a trembly voice. Oh what is it said Ethel.' What it was (as well she knew) was love eternal. Ethel accepts him, faints and is brought back to life by a clever idear of Bernard's, who pours water on her. 'She soon came to and looked up with a sickly smile take me back to the Gaiety hotel she whispered faintly. With plesure my darling said Bernard I will just pack up our viands ere I unloose the boat. Ethel felt better after a few drops of champagne and began to tidy her hair while Bernard packed the remains of the food. Then arm in arm they tottered to the boat. I trust you have not got an illness my darling murmered Bernard as he helped her in. Oh no I am very strong said Ethel I fainted from joy she added to explain matters. Oh I see said Bernard handing her a cushion well some people do he added kindly.'

'So I will end my chapter', the authoress says; and we can picture her doing it complacently, and slowly pulling in her tongue.

Ethel was married in the Abbey. Her wedding dress was 'a rich satin with a humped pattern of gold on the pure white and it had a long train edged with Airum lilies.' 'You will indeed be a charming spectacle my darling gasped Bernard as they left the shop', and I have no doubt she was. She got many delightful presents, the nicest of all being from her father, who 'provided a cheque for £2 and promised to send her a darling little baby calf when ready.' This is perhaps the prettiest touch in the story and should make us all take off our hats to the innocent wondering mind that thought of it.

Poor Mr Salteena. He was at the wedding, dressed in black and crying into his handkerchief. However he recovered to an extent and married Another and had ten children, 'five of each', none of them of course equal to Ethel's children, of whom in a remarkably short time there were seven, which the authoress evidently considers to be the right idear.

It seems to me to be a remarkable work for a child, remarkable even in its length and completeness, for when children turn author they usually stop in the middle, like the kitten when it jumps. The pencilled MS. has been accurately reproduced, not a word added or cut out. Each chapter being in one long paragraph, however, this has been subdivided for the reader's comfort.

J. M. BARRIE

Chap 10th

Preparing for the fray

The next few days were indeed
bussy for Ethel and Bernard
First of all Ethel got some
dainty pink note paper
with silver crest on it
and sent out invitations
in the following terms to
all their freinds.

Miss Ethel Monticue
will be married to Mr
Bernard Clark at
Westminister Abbey on
June 10th. Your company
is requested there at
2-30 sharp and afterwards
for refreshment at the
Gaiety Hotel R. S. V. P.

Having posted heaps of these
and got several replies
Ethel began to order
her wedding dress which
cost a good bit. She chose
a rich satin with a
humped pattern of gold
on the pure white and it
had a long train edged
with arum lilies. Her
veil was of pure lace with
a crown of orange blossom
Her bouquett she ordered
to be of white dog daisies
St Joseph lilies and
orange blossoms tied up
with pale blue satin
ribbon – You will indeed
be a charming spectacle
my darling gasped
Bernard at their

ILLUSTRATOR'S NOTE

As a child, I was fascinated by rouge. My grandmother had a pot, and sometimes she let me and my brothers and sister put it on. It was very agreeable to lounge about the house with a good dob on each cheek. It was natural, then, that when I read *The Young Visiters* at the age of nine, I discovered in Ethel (despite her cavalier treatment of Mr Salteena), a heroine after my own heart, concerning 'ruge'. 'Ruge' was only one of the references to *The Young Visiters* that featured in my own family life: my mother had only to leave the room to go and tidy herself, murmuring 'I shall put some red ruge on my face . . .', for my sister or me to respond '. . . because I am very pale owing to the drains in this house'. Even now, I still have to think twice about spelling 'visitors'.

THE YOUNG VISITERS

Chapter One

QUITE A YOUNG GIRL

MR SALTEENA was an elderly man of 42 and was fond of asking peaple to stay with him. He had quite a young girl staying with him of 17 named Ethel Monticue. Mr Salteena had dark short hair and mustache and wiskers which were very black and twisty. He was middle sized and he had very pale blue eyes. He had a pale brown suit but on Sundays he had a black one and he had a topper every day as he thorght it more becoming. Ethel Monticue had fair hair done on the top and blue eyes. She had a blue velvit frock which had grown rather short in the sleeves. She had a black straw hat and kid gloves.

One morning Mr Salteena came down to brekfast and found Ethel had come down first which was strange.

Is the tea made Ethel he said rubbing his hands. Yes said Ethel and such a quear shaped parcel has come for you. Yes indeed it was a queer shape parcel it was a hat box tied down very tight and a letter stuffed between the string.

1

Well well said Mr Salteena parcels do turn quear I will read the letter first and so saying he tore open the letter and this is what it said

MY DEAR ALFRED.

I want you to come for a stop with me so I have sent you a top hat wraped up in tishu paper inside the box. Will you wear it staying with me because it is very uncommon. Please bring one of your young ladies whichever is the prettiest in the face.

I remain

Yours truely

BERNARD CLARK

Well said Mr Salteena I shall take you to stay Ethel and fancy him sending me a top hat. Then Mr S. opened the box and there lay the most splendid top hat of a lovely rich tone rarther like grapes with a ribbon round compleat.

Well said Mr Salteena peevishly I dont know if I shall like it the bow of the ribbon is too flighty for my age. Then he sat down and eat the egg which Ethel had so kindly laid for him. After he had finished his meal he got down and began to write to Bernard Clark he ran up stairs on his fat legs and took out his blotter with a loud sniff and this is what he wrote

MY DEAR BERNARD

Certinly I shall come and stay with you next Monday I will bring Ethel Montacue commonly called Miss M. She is very active and pretty. I do hope I shall enjoy myself with you. I am fond of digging in the garden and I am parshial to ladies if they are nice I suppose it is my nature. I am not quite a gentleman but you would hardly notice it but cant be helped anyhow. We will come by the 3-15.

Your old and valud friend

ALFRED SALTEENA

Perhaps my readers will be wondering why Bernard Clark had asked Mr Salteena to stay with him. He was a lonely man in a remote spot and he liked peaple and partys but he did not know many. What rot muttered Bernard Clark as he read Mr Salteenas letter. He was rather a presumshious man.

Chapter Two
STARTING GAILY

WHEN the great morning came Mr Salteena did not have an egg for his breakfast in case he should be sick on the jorney.

What top hat will you wear asked Ethel.

I shall wear my best black and my white alpacka coat to keep off the dust and flies replied Mr Salteena.

I shall put some red ruuge on my face said Ethel because I am very pale owing to the drains in this house.

You will look very silly said Mr Salteena with a dry laugh.

Well so will you said Ethel in a snappy tone and she ran out of the room with a very superier run throwing out her legs behind and her arms swinging in rithum.

Well said the owner of the house she has a most idiotick run.

Presently Ethel came back in her best hat and a lovly velvit coat of royal blue. Do I look nice in my get up she asked.

Mr Salteena survayed her. You look rather rash my dear your colors dont quite match your face but never mind I am just going up to say goodbye to Rosalind the housemaid.

Well dont be long said Ethel. Mr S. skipped upstairs to Rosalinds room. Good-bye Rosalind he said I shall be back soon and I hope I shall enjoy myself.

I make no doubt of that sir said Rosalind with a blush as Mr Salteena silently put 2/6 on the dirty toilet cover.

Take care of your bronkitis said Mr S. rather bashfully and he hastilly left the room waving his hand carelessly to the housemaid.

Come along cried Ethel powdering her nose in the hall let us get into the cab. Mr Salteena did not care for powder but he was an unselfish man so he dashed into the cab. Sit down said Ethel as the cabman waved his whip you are standing on my luggage. Well I am paying for the cab said Mr S. so I might be allowed to put my feet were I like.

They traveled 2nd class in the train and Ethel was longing to go first but thought perhaps least said soonest mended. Mr Salteena got very excited in the train about his visit. Ethel was calm but she felt excited inside. Bernard has a big house said Mr S. gazing at Ethel he is inclined to be rich.

Oh indeed said Ethel looking at some cows flashing past the window. Mr S. felt rather disheartened so he read the paper till the train stopped and the porters shouted Rickamere station. We had better collect our traps said Mr Salteena and just then a very exalted footman in a cocked hat and olive green uniform put his head in at the window. Are you for Rickamere Hall he said in impressive tones.

Well yes I am said Mr Salteena and so is this lady.

Very good sir said the noble footman if you will alight I will see to your luggage there is a convayance awaiting you.

Oh thankyou thankyou said Mr S. and he and Ethel stepped along the platform. Outside they found a lovely cariage lined with olive green cushions to match the footman and the horses had green bridles and bows on their manes and tails. They got gingerly in. Will he bring our luggage asked Ethel nervously.

I expect so said Mr Salteena lighting a very long cigar.

Do we tip him asked Ethel quietly.

Well no I dont think so not yet we had better just thank him perlitely.

Just then the footman staggered out with the bagage. Ethel bowed gracefuly over the door of the cariage and Mr S. waved his hand as each bit of luggage was hoisted up to make sure it was all there. Then he said thankyou my good fellow very politely. Not at all sir said the footman and touching his cocked hat he jumped actively to the box.

I was right not to tip him whispered Mr Salteena the thing to do is to leave 2/6 on your dressing table when your stay is over.

Does he find it asked Ethel who did not really know at all how to go on at a visit. I beleeve so replied Mr Salteena anyhow it is quite the custom and we cant help it if he does not. Now my dear what do you think of the sceenery.

Very nice said Ethel gazing at the rich fur rug on her knees. Just then the cariage rolled into a beautifull drive with tall trees and big red flowers growing amid shiny dark leaves. Presently the haughty coachman pulled up with a great clatter at a huge front door with tall pillers each side a big iron bell and two very clean scrapers. The doors flung open as if by majic causing Ethel to jump and a portly butler appeared on the scene with a very shiny shirt front and a huge pale face. Welcome sir he exclaimed good naturedly as Mr Salteena alighted rather quickly from the viacle and please to step inside.

Mr Salteena stepped in as bid followed by Ethel. The footman again struggled with the luggage and the butler Francis Minnit by name kindly lent a hand. The hall was very big and hung round with guns and mats and ancestors giving it a gloomy but a grand air. The butler then showed them down a winding corridoor till he came to a door which he flung open shouting Mr Salteena and a lady sir.

A tall man of 29 rose from the sofa. He was rather bent in the middle with very nice long legs fairish hair and blue eyes. Hullo Alf old boy he cried so you have got here all safe and no limbs broken.

None thankyou Bernard replied Mr Salteena shaking hands and let me introduce Miss Monticue she is very pleased to come for this visit.

Oh yes gasped Ethel blushing through her red ruuge.

Bernard looked at her keenly and turned a dark red. I am glad to see you he said I hope you will enjoy it but I have not arranged any partys yet as I dont know anybody.

Dont worry murmered Ethel I dont mix much in Socierty and she gave him a dainty smile.

I expect you would like some tea said Bernard I will ring.

Yes indeed we should said Mr Salteena egerly.

Bernard pealed on the bell and the butler came in with a stately walk.

Tea please Minnit crid Bernard Clark. With pleasure sir replied Minnit with a deep bow. A glorious tea then came in on a gold tray two kinds of bread and butter a lovly jam role and lots of sugar cakes. Ethels eyes began to sparkle and she made several remarks during the meal. I expect you would now like to unpack said Bernard when it was over.

Well yes that is rarther an idear said Mr Salteena.

I have given the best spare room to Miss Monticue said Bernard with a gallant bow and yours turning to Mr Salteena opens out of it so you will be nice and friendly both the rooms have big windows and a handsome view.

How charming said Ethel. Yes well let us go up replied Bernard and he led the way up many a winding stairway till they came to an oak door with some lovly swans and bull rushes painted on it. Here we are he cried gaily. Ethels room was indeed a handsome compartment with purple silk curtains and a 4 post bed draped with the same shade. The toilit set was white and mauve and there were some violets in a costly varse. Oh I say cried Ethel in supprise. I am glad you like it said Bernard and here we have yours Alf. He opened the dividing door and portrayed a smaller but dainty room in all pale yellow and wild primroses. My own room is next the bath room said Bernard it is decerated dark red as I have somber tastes. The bath room has got a tip up baison and a hose thing for washing your head.

9

A good notion said Mr Salteena who was secretly getting jellus. Here we will leave our friends to unpack and end this Chapter.

Chapter Three

THE FIRST EVENING

WHEN they had unpacked Mr Salteena and Ethel went downstairs to dinner. Mr Salteena had put on a complete evening suit as he thought it was the correct idear and some ruby studs he had got at a sale. Ethel had on a dress of yellaw silk covered with tulle which was quite in the fashion and she had on a necklace which Mr Salteena gave her for a birthday present. She looked very becomeing and pretty and Bernard heaved a sigh as he gave her his arm to go into dinner. The butler Minnit was quite ready for the fray standing up very stiff and surrounded by two footmen in green plush and curly white wigs who were called Charles and Horace.

Well said Mr Salteena lapping up his turtle soup you have a very sumpshous house Bernard.

His friend gave a weary smile and swallowed a few drops of sherry wine it is fairly decent he replied with a bashful glance at Ethel after our repast I will show you over the premisis.

Many thanks said Mr Salteena getting rather flustered with his forks.

You ourght to give a ball remarked Ethel you have such large compartments.

Yes there is room enough sighed Bernard we might try a few steps and meanwhile I might get to know a few peaple.

So you might responded Ethel giving him a speaking look.

Mr Salteena was growing a little peevish but he cheered up when the Port wine came on the table and the butler put round some costly finger bowls. He did not have any in his own house and he followed Bernard Clarks advice as to what to do with them. After dinner Ethel played some merry tunes on the piano and Bernard responded with a rather loud song in a base voice and Ethel clapped him a good deal. Then Mr Salteena asked a few riddles as he was not musical. Then Bernard said shall I show you over my domain and they strolled through the gloomy hall.

I see you have a lot of ancesters said Mr Salteena in a jelous tone, who are they.

Well said Bernard they are all quite correct. This is my aunt Caroline she was rather exentrick and quite old.

So I see said Mr Salteena and he passed on to a lady with a very tight waist and quearly shaped. That is Mary Anne Fudge my grandmother I think said Bernard she was very well known in her day.

Why asked Ethel who was rather curious by nature.

Well I dont quite know said Bernard but she was and he moved away to the next picture. It was of a man with a fat smiley face and a red ribbon round him and a lot of medals. My great uncle Ambrose Fudge said Bernard carelessly.

He looks a thourough ancester said Ethel kindly.

Well he was said Bernard in a proud tone he was really the Sinister son of Queen Victoria.

Not really cried Ethel in excited tones but what does that mean.

Well I dont quite know said Bernard Clark it puzzles me very much but ancesters do turn quear at times.

Perhaps it means god son said Mr Salteena in an inteligent voice.

Well I dont think so said Bernard but I mean to find out.

It is very grand anyhow said Ethel.

It is that replied her host genially.

Who is this said Mr Salteena halting at a picture of a lady holding up some grapes and smiling a good deal.

Her name was called Minnie Pilato responded Bernard she was rather far back but a real relation and she was engaged to the earl of Tullyvarden only it did not quite come off.

What a pity crid Ethel.

Yes it was rather replied Bernard but she marrid a Captain in the Navy and had seven children so she was quite alright.

Here Mr Salteena thourght he had better go to bed as he had had a long jorney. Bernard always had a few prayers in the hall and some whiskey afterwards as he was rather pious but Mr Salteena was not very adicted to prayers so he marched up to bed. Ethel stayed as she thought it would be a good thing. The butler came in as he was a very holy man and Bernard piously said the Our Father and a very good hymn called I will keep my anger down and a Decad of the Rosary. Ethel chimed in quiutly and Francis Minnit was most devout and Ethel thought what a good holy family she was stopping with. So I will end my chapter.

Chapter Four

MR SALTEENAS PLAN

MR SALTEENA woke up rather early next day and was supprised and delighted to find Horace the footmen entering with a cup of tea.

Oh thankyou my man said Mr Salteena rolling over in the costly bed.

Mr Clarke is nearly out of the bath sir anounced Horace I will have great plesure in turning it on for you if such is your desire. Well yes you might said Mr Salteena seeing it was the idear and Horace gave a profound bow.

Ethel are you getting up shouted Mr Salteena.

Very nearly replied Ethel faintly from the next room.

I say said Mr Salteena excitedly I have had some tea in bed.

So have I replied Ethel.

Then Mr Salteena got into a mauve dressing gaun with yellaw tassles and siezing his soap he wandered off to the bath room which was most sumpshous. It had a lovly white shiny bath and sparkling taps and several towels arrayed in readiness by thourght-ful Horace. It also had a step for climbing up the bath and other good dodges of a rich nature. Mr Salteena washed himself well and felt very much better.

After brekfast Mr Salteena asked Bernard if he could have some private conversation with him. Well yes replied Bernard if you will come into my study we can have a few words.

Cant I come too muttered Ethel sulkily.

No my dear said Mr Salteena this is privite.

Perhaps later I might have a private chat with you Miss Montacue said Bernard kindly.

Oh do lets said Ethel.

Then Bernard and Mr S. strolled to the study and sat upon two arm chairs. Fire away said Bernard lighting his pipe.

Well I cant exactly do that said Mr Salteena in slow tones it is a searious matter and you can advise me as you are a thorugh gentleman I am sure.

Well yes said Bernard what can I do for you eh Alf?

You can help me perhaps to be more like a gentleman said Mr Salteena getting rather hot I am quite alright as they say but I would like to be the real thing can it be done he added slapping his knees.

I dont quite know said Bernard it might take a good time.

Might it said Mr S. but I would slave for years if need be. Bernard scratched his head. Why dont you try the Crystal Pallace he asked several peaple Earls and even dukes have private compartments there.

But I am not an Earl said Mr Salteena in a purplexed tone.

16

True replied Bernard but I understand there are sort of students there who want to get into the War Office and notable banks.

Would that be a help asked Mr Salteena egerly.

Well it might said Bernard I can give you a letter to my old pal the earl of Clincham who lives there he might rub you up and by mixing with him you would probably grow more seemly.

Oh ten thousand thanks said Mr Salteena I will go there as soon as it can be arranged if you would be so kind as to keep an eye on Ethel while I am away.

Oh yes said Bernard I may be running up to town for a few days and she could come too.

You are too kind said Mr Salteena and I dont think you will find her any trouble.

No I dont think I shall said Bernard she is a pretty girl cheerful and active and he blushed rather red.

Chapter Five

THE CRYSTAL PALACE

About 9 oclock next morning Mr Salteena stood bag in hand in the ancestle hall waiting for the viacle to convay him to the station. Bernard Clarke and Ethel were seated side by side on a costly sofa gazing abstractly at the parting guest. Horace had dashed off to put on his cocked hat as he was going in the barouche but Francis Minnit was roaming about the hall well prepared for any deed.

Well said Bernard puffing at his meershum pipe I hope you will get on Alf I am sure you have that little letter to old Clincham eh.

Indeed I have said Mr Salteena many thanks for the same and I do hope Ethel will behave properly.

Oh yes I expect she will said Bernard with a sigh.

I always do said Ethel in a snappy tone.

Just then there was a great clatter outside and the sound of hoofs and a loud neigh. The barouche I take it said Bernard rising slowly.

Quite correct sir said Minnit flinging wide the portalls.

Well goodbye Alf old man said Bernard Clarke good luck and God bless you he added in a pius tone.

Not at all said Mr Salteena I have enjoyed my stop which has been short and sweet well goodbye Ethel my child he said as bag in hand he proceeded to the door. Francis Minnit bowed low and handed a small parcel to Mr Salteena a few sandwighs for the jorney sir he remarked.

Oh this is most kind said Mr Salteena.

Minnit closed his eyes with a tired smile. Not kind sir he muttered quite usual.

Oh really said Mr Salteena feeling rarther flabergasted well goodbye my good fellow and he slipped 2/6d into the butlers open palm.

Mr Salteena had to travel first class as active Horace ran on to buy the ticket which he presented with a low bow the Times and TitBits. Oh many thanks my man said Mr Salteena in a most airy voice now will you find me a comer seat in the train eh.

19

If there is one sir replied Horace.

In got Mr Salteena to his first class carriage surrounded by his baggage carefully piled up by kindly Horace. The other pasengers looked full of envy at the curly white wig and green plush uniform of Horace. Mr Salteena crossed his legs in a lordly way and flung a fur rug over his knees though he was hot enough in all consciunce. He began to feel this was the thin end of the partition and he smiled as he gently tapped the letter in his coat tail pocket. When Mr Salteena arrived in London he began to strolle up the principle streets thinking how gay all was. Presently he beheld a resterant with a big Menu outside and he went boldly in.

It was a sumpshous spot all done up in gold and plenty of looking glasses. Meny handsome ladies and gentlemen were already partaking of choice food and rich wines and whisky and the scene was most lively. Mr Salteena had a little whiskey to make him feel more at home. Then he eat some curry to the tune of a merry valse on the band. He beat time to the music and smiled kindly at the waiters and he felt very excited inside. I am seeing life with a vengance he muttered to himself as he paid his bill at the desk. Outside Mr Salteena found a tall policeman. Could you direct me to the Crystal pallace if you please said Mr Salteena nervously.

Well said the geniul policeman my advice would be to take a cab sir.

Oh would it said Mr Salteena then I will do so.

He hailed a hansome and got speedily in to the crystal palace he cried gaily and holding his bag on his knees he prepared to enjoy the sights of the metropilis. It was a merry drive and all too soon the Palace heaved in view. Mr Salteena sprang out and paid the man then he entered the wondrous edifice. His heart beat very fast as two huge men in gold braid flung open the doors. Inside was a lovely fountain in the middle and all round were little stalls where you could buy sweets and lemonade also scent hankerchiefs and many dainty articles. There were a lot of people but nobody very noteable.

At last after buying two bottles of scent and some rather nice sweets which stuck to his teeth Mr Salteena beheld a wooden door on which was nailed a notice saying To the Private Compartments.

Ah ha said Mr Salteena to himself this is evidently my next move, and he gently pushed open the door straitening his top hat as he did so. Inside he found himself in a dimly lit passage with a thick and handsome carpet. Mr Salteena gazed round and beheld in the gloom a very superier gentleman in full evening dress who was reading a newspaper and warming his hands on the hot water pipes. Mr Salteena advanced on tiptoe and coughed gently as so far the gentleman had paid no attention. However at the second cough he raised his eyes in a weary fashion, do you want anything he asked in a most noble voice.

Mr Salteena got very flustered. Well I am seeking the earl of Clincham he began in a trembly voice, are you by any chance him he added most respectfully.

No not exacktly replied the other my name happens to be Edward Procurio. I am half italian and I am the Groom of the Chambers.

What chambers asked Mr Salteena blinking his eyes.

These said Edward Procurio waving a thin arm.

Mr Salteena then noticed several red doors with names of people on each one. Oh I see he said then perhaps you can tell me where the earl of Clincham is to be found.

At the end of the passage fourth door down said Procurio tritely of course he may be out one never knows what they are up to.

I suppose not said Mr Salteena in an interested tone.

One can not gamble on anything really said Procurio returning to the hot water pipes though of course I know a lot more than most people about the inmates here.

What are the habits of the earl of Clincham said Mr Salteena.

Procurio gave a smile many and varius he replied I cant say much in my position but one lives and learns. He heaved a sigh and shruged his shoulders.

Well good day said Mr Salteena feeling better for the chat.

Procurio nodded in silence as Mr Salteena trotted off down the passage. At last he came to a door labelled Clincham Earl of in big letters. With a beating heart Mr Salteena pulled the bell and the door swung open of its own accord. At the same moment a cheery voice rang out from the distance. Come in please I am in the study first door on left.

With a nervous bound Mr Salteena obeyd these directions and found himself in a small but handsome compartment done in dark green lether with crests on the chairs. Over the mantlepiece was hung the painting of a lady in a low neck looking quite the thing. By the desk was seated a tall man of 35 with very nice eyes of a twinkly nature and curly hair he wore a quite plain suit of palest grey but well made and on the table reposed a grey top hat which had evidently been on his head recently. He had a rose in his button hole also a signet ring.

Hullo said this plesant fellow as Mr Salteena was spell bound on mat.

Hullo your Lord Ship responded our hero bowing low and dropping his top hat do I adress the earl of Clincham.

You do said the Earl with a homely smile and who do I adress eh.

Our hero bowed again Alfred Salteena he said in deep tones.

Oh I see said the kindly earl well come in my man and tell me who you are.

Mr Salteena seated himself gingerly on the edge of a crested chair.

To tell you the truth my Lord I am not anyone of import and I am not a gentleman as they say he ended getting very red and hot.

Have some whisky said lord Clincham and he poured the liquid into a glass at his elbow. Mr Salteena lapped it up thankfully.

Well my man said the good natured earl what I say is what dose it matter we cant all be of the Blood royal can we.

No said Mr Salteena but I suppose you are.

Lord Clincham waved a careless hand. A small portion flows in my viens he said but it does not worry me at all and after all he added piously at the Day of Judgement what will be the odds.

Mr Salteena heaved a sigh. I was thinking of this world he said.

Oh I see said the earl but my own idear is that these things are as piffle before the wind.

Not being an earl I cant say answered our hero but may I beg you to read this letter my Lord. He produced Bernards note from his coat tails. The earl of Clincham took it in his long fingers. This is what he read.

My dear Clincham
The bearer of this letter is an old friend of mine not quite the right side of the blanket as they say in fact he is the son of a first rate butcher but his mother was a decent family called Hyssopps of the Glen so you see he is not so bad and is desireus of being

the correct article. Could you rub him up a bit in socierty ways. I dont know much details about him but no doubt he will supply all you need.

I am keeping well and hope you are. I must run up to the Compartments one day and look you up.

Yours as ever your faithfull friend

BERNARD CLARKE

The earl gave a slight cough and gazed at Mr Salteena thourghtfully have you much money he asked and are you prepared to spend a good deal.

Oh yes quite gasped Mr Salteena I have plenty in the bank and £10 in ready gold in my purse.

You see these compartments are the haunts of the aristockracy said the earl and they are kept going by peaple who have got something funny in their family and who want to be less mere if you can comprehend.

Indeed I can said Mr Salteena.

Personally I am a bit parshial to mere people said his Lordship but the point is that we charge a goodly sum for our training here but however if you cant pay you need not join.

I can and will proclaimed Mr Salteena and he placed a £10 note on the desk. His lordship slipped it in his trouser pocket. It will be £42 before I have done with you he said but you can pay me here and there as convenient.

Oh thankyou cried Mr Salteena.

Not at all said the earl and now to bissness. While here you will live in compartments in the basement known as Lower Range. You will get many hints from the Groom of the Chambers as to clothes and ettiquett to menials. You will mix with me for grammer and I might take you out hunting or shooting sometimes to give you a few tips. Also I have lots of ladies parties which you will attend occasionally.

Mr Salteenas eyes flashed with excitement. I shall enjoy that he cried.

His Lordship coughed loudly you may not marry while under instruction he said firmly.

Oh I shall not need to thank you said Mr Salteena.

You must also decide on a profeshion said his Lordship as your instruction will vary according.

Could I be anything at Buckingham pallace said Mr Salteena with flashing eyes.

Oh well I dont quite know said the noble earl but you might perhaps gallopp beside the royal barouche if you care to try.

Oh indeed I should cried Mr Salteena I am very fond of fresh air and royalties.

Well said the earl with a knowing smile I might arrange it with the prince of Wales who I am rarther intimate with.

Not really gasped Mr Salteena.

Dear me yes remarked the earl carelessly and if we decide for you to gallopp by the royal viacle you must be mesured for some plush knickerbockers at once.

Mr Salteena glanced at his rarther fat legs and sighed.

Well I must go out now and call on a few Dowagers said his Lordship picking up his elegent top hat. Well au revoir he added with a good french accent.

Adieu my Lord crid Mr Salteena not to be out done we meet anon I take it.

Not till tomorrow answered the earl you will now proceed to the lower regions where you will no doubt find tea. He nodded kindly and glided out in silence.

Here I will end my chapter.

Chapter Six

HIGH LIFE

MR SALTEENA awoke next morning in his small but pleasant room. It was done in green and white with Monagrams on the toilit set. He had a tiny white bed with a green quilt and a picture of the Nativaty and one of Windsor Castle on the walls. The sun was shining over all these things as Mr Salteena opened his sleepy eyes. Just then there was a rat tat on the door. Come in called Mr Salteena and in came Edward Procurio ballancing a tray very cleverly. He looked most elegant with his shiny black hair and pale yellow face and half shut eyes. He smiled in a very mysterious and superier way as he placed the tray on Mr Salteenas pointed knees.

Your early beverage he announced and began to pull up the blinds still smiling to himself.

Oh thankyou cried Mr Salteena feeling very towzld compared to this grand fellow. Then to his great supprise Procurio began to open the wardrobe and look at Mr Salteenas suits making italian exclamations under his breath. Mr Salteena dare not say a word so he swollowed his tea and eat a Marie biscuit hastilly. Presently

Procurio advanced to the bed with a bright blue serge suit. Will you wear this today sir he asked quietly.

Oh certainly said Mr Salteena.

And a clean shirt would not come amiss said Procurio what about this pale blue and white stripe.

With pleashure replied Mr Salteena. So Procurio laid them out in neat array also a razer and brush for shaving. Then he opened a door saying this is the bath room shall I turn on hot or cold.

I dont mind said Mr Salteena feeling very hot and ignorant.

It is best for you to decide sir said Procurio firmly.

Well I will try cold said Mr Salteena feeling it was more manly to say that. Procurio bowed and beat a retreat to the bath room. Then he returned and told Mr Salteena that when he was washed he would find his breakfast in the sitting room. When Mr Salteena was dressed in his best blue suit and clean shirt he stroled into the sitting room where a gay canary was singing fit to burst in the window and a copple of doves cooing in a whicker cage. A cheery smell greeted him as Procurio glided in with some steaming coffie. Mr Salteena felt more at home and passed a few remarks about the weather. Procurio smiled and uncovered some lovely kidnys on toast and as he did so bent and whispered in Mr Salteenas ears you could have come in in your dressing gown.

Mr Salteena gave a start. Oh can I he said ten thousand thanks.

Then Procurio passed out and Mr Salteena furnished his kidneys and chiruped to the birds and had a cigarette from a handsome purple box which he found on the desk. Then Procurio entered once more and with a bow said. His lordship is going to a levie this morning and thinks it might amuse you to go too. Could you be ready by 11 oclock.

Oh yes what fun said Mr Salteena have you any notion what a levie is my man.

Procurio gave a superier smile. It is a party given by the Queen to very superier peaple but this one is given by the Prince of Wales as the Queen is not quite her usual self today. It will be at Buckingham palace so you will drive with his lordship.

Mr Salteena was fearfully excited. What shall I weare he gasped.

Well of course you ought to have black satin knickerbockers and a hat with white feathers also garters and a star or two.

You supprise me said Mr Salteena I have none of those articles.

Well said Procurio kindly his lordship will lend you his second best cocked hat as you are obliged to wear one and I think with a little thourght I might rig you up so as to pass muster.

Then they rumaged among Mr Salteenas things and Procurio got very intelligent and advised Mr Salteena to wear his black evening suit and roll up his trousers. He also lent him a pair of white silk stockings which he fastened tighdy round his knees with red rosettes. Then he quickly cut out a star in silver paper and pinned it to his chest and also added a strip of red ribbon across his shirt front. Then Mr Salteena survayed himself in the glass. Is it a fancy dress party he asked – no they always wear that kind of thing but wait till you see his lordship – if you are ready sir I will conduct you in.

Mr Salteena followed Procurio up countless stairs till they came to the earls compartments and tapped on the bedroom door.

Come in cried a merry voice and in they strode.

I have done my best with Mr Salteena my lord I trust he will do the hat of course will make a deal of difference.

Mr Salteena bowed nervously wishing he had got correct knickerboccers as his trousers did not feel too firm in spite of the garters.

Not half bad cried the earl try on the hat Salteena it is on my bed. Mr Salteena placed it on his head and the feathers and gold braid became him very well but he felt very jellous of the earl who looked a sight for the gods. He had proper satin knickerbockers with diamond clasps and buckled shoes and black silk stockings which showed up his long fine legs. He had a floppy shirt of soft-ist muslin with real lace collar and cuffs. A sword hung at his side and a crimson sash was round his waist and a splendid cocked hat on his head. His blue eyes twinkled as he pulled on a pair of white kid gloves.

Well come on Salteena he cried and dont be nervus I will get you a pair of knickers tomorrow. Will you get a hansome Procurio.

Presently the earl and Mr Salteena were clattering away to Buckingham palace.

You wont mind if I introduce you as Lord Hyssops do you said the earl as he lit his pipe. You see you are sort of mixed up with the family so it wont matter and will look better.

So it would said Mr Salteena what do we do at the levie.

Oh we strole round and eat ices and champaigne and that kind of thing and sometimes there is a little music.

Is there any dancing asked Mr Salteena.

Well not always said the earl.

I am glad of that said Mr Salteena I am not so nimble as I was and my garters are a trifle tight.

Sometimes we talk about the laws and politics said the earl if Her Majesty is in that kind of mood.

Just then the splendid edifice appeared in view and Mr Salteena licked his dry lips at the sight of the vast crowd. All round were carrages full of costly peaple and outside the railings stood tall Life Guards keeping off the mere peaple who had gathered to watch the nobility clatter up. Lord Clincham began to bow right and left raising his cocked hat to his friends. There was a lot of laughter and friendly words as the cab finally drew up at the front door. Two tall life guards whisked open the doors and one of them kindly tipped the cabman. Mr Salteena followed his lordship up the grand steps trying to feel as homely as he could. Then a splendid looking fellow in a red tunick and a sort of black velvit tam a shanter stepped forward from the throng shouting what name please.

The Earl of Clincham and Lord Hyssops calmly replied the earl gently nudging Mr Salteena to act up. Mr Salteena nodded and blinked at the menial as much as to say all is well and then he and the earl hung up their cocked hats on two pegs. This way cried a deep voice and another menial appeared wearing stiff white britches top boots and a green velvit coat with a leather belt also a very shiny top hat. They followed this fellow down countless corridors and finally came to big folding doors. The earl twiddled his mustache and slapped his leg with his white glove as calmly as could be. Mr Salteena purspired rather hard and gave a hitch to his garters to make sure.

Then the portals divided and their names were shouted in chorus by countless domestics. The sumshious room was packed with men of a noble nature dressed like the earl in satin knickerboccers etc. and with ladies of every hue with long trains and jewels by the dozen. You could hardly moove in the gay throng. Dukes were as nought as there were a good lot of princes and Arch dukes as it was a very superier levie indeed. The earl and Mr Salteena struggled through the crowd till they came to a platform draped with white velvit. Here on a golden chair was seated the prince of Wales in a lovely ermine cloak and a small but costly crown. He was chatting quite genially with some of the crowd.

Up clambered the earl followed at top speed by Mr Salteena.

Hullo Clincham cried the Prince quite homely and not at all grand so glad you turned up – quite a squash eh.

A bit over powering your Highness said the earl who was quite used to all this may I introduce my friend Lord Hyssops he is staying with me so I thought I would bring him along if you dont mind Prince.

Not at all cried the genial prince looking rather supprised. Mr Salteena bowed so low he nearly fell off the platform and as the prince put out a hand Mr Salteena thought he had better kiss it. The Prince smiled kindly I am pleased to see you Lord Hyssops he said in a regal voice.

Then the Earl chipped in and how is the dear Queen he said reveruntly.

Not up to much said his Highness she feels the heat poor soul and he waved to a placard which said in large letters. The Queen is indisposed.

Presently his Highness rose I think I will have a quiet glass of champaigne he said you come too Clincham and bring your friend the Diplomats are arriving and I am not much in the mood for deep talk I have already signed a dozen documents so I have done my duty.

They all went out by a private door and found themselves in a smaller but gorgous room. The Prince tapped on the table and instantly two menials in red tunics appeared. Bring three glasses of champaigne commanded the prince and some ices he added majestikally. The goods appeared as if by majic and the prince drew out a cigar case and passed it round.

One grows weary of Court Life he remarked.

Ah yes agreed the earl.

It upsets me said the prince lapping up his strawberry ice all I want is peace and quiut and a little fun and here I am tied down to this life he said taking off his crown being royal has many painfull drawbacks.

True mused the earl.

Silence fell and the strains of the band could be heard from the next room. Suddenly the prince gazed at Mr Salteena. Who did you say you were he asked in a puzzled tone.

Lord Hyssops responded our hero growing purple at the lie.

Well you are not a bit like the Lord Hyssops I know replied the prince could you explain matters.

Mr Salteena gazed helplessly at the earl who had grown very pale and seemed lost for the moment. However he quickly recovered.

He is quite alright really Prince he said. His mother was called Miss Hyssops of the Glen.

Indeed said his royal Highness that sounds correct but who was your father eh.

Then Mr Salteena thourght he would not tell a lie so in trembly tones he muttered my poor father was but a butcher your Highness a very honest one I may add and passing rich he was called Domonic Salteena and my name is Alfred Salteena.

The Prince stroked his yellow beard and rarther admired Mr Salteena for his truthful utterance – Oh I see he said well why did you palm off on my menials as Lord Hyssops eh.

Mr Salteena wiped his swetting brow but the earl came to the rescue nobly. My fault entirely Prince he chimed in as I was bringing him to this very supearier levie I thought it would be better to say he was of noble birth have I offended your Royal dignity.

Not much said the prince it was a laudible notion and perhaps I will ask Mr Salteena to one of my big balls some day.

Oh your Highness gasped our hero falling on one knee that would indeed be a treat.

I suppose Prince you have not got a job going at this palace for my friend asked the earl you see I am rubbing him up in socierty ways and he fancies court life as a professhon.

Oh dose he said the prince blinking his eyes well I might see.

I suggested if there was a vacancy going he might try cantering after the royal barouche said the earl.

So he might said the prince I will speak to the prime Minister about it and let you know.

Ten thousand thanks cried Mr Salteena bowing low.

Well now I must get along back to the levie announced the prince putting on his crown I have booked a valse with the Arch duchess of Greenwich and this is her favorite tune. So saying they issued back to the big room where the nobility were whirling gaily and the more searius peaple such as the prime minister and the admirals etc were eating ices and talking passionately about the laws in a low undertone.

The earl was soon mingling gaily in a set of lancers but Mr Salteena dare not because of his trousers. However he sat on a velvit chair and quite enjoyed over hearing the intelligent conversation of the prime minister. And now we will leave our hero enjoying his glimpse of high life and return to Ethel Montacue.

Chapter Seven
BERNARDS IDEAR

AFTER Mr Salteena had departed Bernard Clark thought he would show Ethel over his house so they spent a merry morning so doing. Ethel passed bright remarks on all the rooms and Bernard thought she was most pretty and Ethel began to be a bit excited. After a lovly lunch they sat in the gloomy hall and Ethel began to feel very glad Mr Salteena was not there. Suddenly Bernard lit his pipe I was thinking he said passionately what about going up to London for a weeks Gaierty.

Who inquired Ethel in a low tone.

You and me said Bernard I know of several splendid hotels and we could go to theaters and parties and enjoy ourselves to the full.

So we could what an idear cried Ethel.

So the merry plan was all arranged and they spent the afternoon in packing their trunks. Next day they were all ready in the hall when the handsome viacle once more clattered up. Ethel had on her blue velvit get up and a sweet new hat and plenty of ruge on her face and looked quite a seemly counterpart for Bernard who was arrayed in a white and shiny mackintosh top boots and a well brushed top hat tied on to him with a bit of black elastick.

Well goodbye Minnit he cried to the somber butler take care of your gout and the silver and I will pay your wages when I come back.

Thank you kindly sir murmered Minnit when may I expect your return.

Oh well I will wire he said and dashed doun the steps.

Ethel followed with small lady like steps having bowed perlitely to Minnit who closed his eyes in acknowlegment of her kindness.

The sun was shining and Ethel had the feeling of going to a very jolly party and felt so sorry for all the passers by who were not going to London with Bernard.

Arrived in the gay city Bernard hailed a cab to the manner born and got in followed by Ethel. Kindly drive us to the Gaierty Hotel he cried in a firm tone. The cabman waved his whip and off they dashed.

We shall be highly comfortable and select at the Gaiety said Bernard and he thought to himself how lovly it would be if he was married to Ethel. He blushed a deep shade at his own thoughts and gave a side long glance at Ethel who was gazing out of the window. Well one never knows he murmered to himself and as one of the poets says great events from trivil causes springs.

Just then they stopped at the gay hotel and Ethel was spellbound at the size of the big hall — Bernard poked his head into the window of the pay desk. Have you a coupple of bedrooms for self and young lady he enquired in a lordly way.

A very handsome lady with golden hair and a lace apron glanced at a book and hastily replied Oh yes sir two beauties on the 1st floor number 9 and 10.

Thankyou said Bernard we will go up if you have no objection.

None whatever sir said the genial lady the beds are well aired and the view is quite pleasant.

Come along Ethel cried Bernard this sounds alright eh.

Oh quite said Ethel with a beaming smile.

They went upstairs and entered no 9 a very fine compartment with a large douny bed and white doors with glass handles leading into no: 10 an equally dainty room but a trifle smaller.

Which will you have Ethel asked Bernard.

Oh well I would rather you settled it said Ethel. I am willing to abide by your choice.

The best shall be yours then said Bernard bowing gallantly and pointing to the biggest room.

Ethel blushed at his speaking look. I shall be quite lost in that huge bed she added to hide her embarassment.

Yes I expect you will said Bernard and now what about a little table d'ote followed by a theater.

Oh yes cried Ethel and downstairs they went.

Chapter Eight

A GAY CALL

I TELL you what Ethel said Bernard Clarke about a week later we might go and pay a call on my pal the earl of Clincham.

Oh do lets cried Ethel who was game for any new adventure I would dearly love to meet his Lordship.

Bernard gave a frown of jellousy at her rarther mere words.

Well dress in your best he muttered.

Ethel skipped into her bedroom and arrayd herself in a grass green muslin of decent cut a lace scarf long faun colored kid gloves and a muslin hat to correspond. She carried a parasole in one hand also a green silk bag containing a few stray hair pins a clean handkerchief five shillings and a pot of ruge in case. She looked a dainty vishen with her fair hair waving in the breeze and Bernard bit his lips rather hard for he could hardly contain himself and felt he must marry Ethel soon. He looked a handsome sight himself in some exquisite white trousers with a silk shirt and a pale blue blazer belt and cap. He wore this in honour of the earl who had been to Cambridge in his youth and so had Bernard Clark.

At last they found themselves in the entrance hall of the Crystale palace and speedily made their way to the private compartments. Edward Procurio was walking up and down the passage looking dark and mysterious as usual.

Is His Lordship at home cried Bernard Clarke cheerily.

Which one asked Procurio many lords live here he said scornfully.

Well I mean the earl of Clincham said Bernard.

Oh yes he is in responded Procurio and to the best of my belief giving a party.

Indeed ejaculated Bernard we have come in the nick of time Ethel he added. Yes said Ethel in an excited tone.

Then they pealed on the bell and the door flew open. Sounds of laughter and comic songs issued from the abode and in a second they were in the crowded drawing room. It was packed with all the elite and a stout duchess with a good natured face was singing a lively song and causing much merriment. The earl strode forward at sight of two new comers. Hullo Bernard old boy he cried this is a pleasure and who have you got with you he added glancing at Ethel.

Oh this is Miss Montacue said Bernard shall I introduce you—

If you will be so good said the earl in an affable tone and Bernard hastilly performed the right. Ethel began a bright conversation while Bernard stroled off to see if he could find any friends amid the throng.

44

What plesant compartments you have cried Ethel in rarther a socierty tone.

Fairly so so responded the earl do you live in London he added in a loud tone as someone was playing a very difficult piece on the piano.

Well no I dont said Ethel my home is really in Northumberland but I am at present stopping with Mr Clark at the Gaierty Hotel she continued in a somewhat showing off tone.

Oh I see said the earl well shall I introduce you to a few of my friends.

Oh please do said Ethel with a dainty blow at her nose.

The earl disserppeard into the madding crowd and presently came back with a middle aged gentleman. This is Lord Hyssops he said my friend Miss Montacue he added genially.

Ethel turned a dull yellaw. Lord Hyssops she said in a faint voice why it is Mr Salteena I know him well.

Hush cried the earl it is a title bestowed recently by my friend the Prince of Wales.

Yes indeed murmered Mr Salteena deeply flabbergasted by the ready wit of the earl.

Oh indeed said Ethel in a peevish tone well how do you come to be here.

I am stopping with his Lordship said Mr Salteena and have a set of compartments in the basement so there.

I dont care said huffy Ethel I am in handsome rooms at the Gaierty.

Nothing could be nicer I am sure struck in the earl what do you say Hyssops eh.

Doubtless it is charming said Mr Salteena who was wanting peace tell me Ethel how did you leave Bernard.

I have not left him said Ethel in an annoying voice I am stopping with him at the gaierty and we have been to lots of theaters and dances.

Well I am glad you are enjoying yourself said Mr Salteena kindly you had been looking pale of late.

No wonder in your stuffy domain cried Ethel well have you got any more friends she added turning to the earl.

Well I will see said the obliging earl and he once more disapeared.

I dont know why you should turn against me Ethel said Mr Salteena in a low tone.

Ethel patted her hair and looked very sneery. Well I call it very mysteareous you going off and getting a title said Ethel and I think our friendship had better stop as no doubt you will soon be marrying a duchess or something.

Not at all said Mr Salteena you must know Ethel he said blushing a deep red I always wished to marry you some fine day.

This is news to me cried Ethel still peevish.

But not to me murmered Mr Salteena and his voice trembled in his chest. I may add that I have always loved you and now I seem to do so madly he added passionately.

But I dont love you responded Ethel.

But if you married me you might get to said Mr Salteena.

I think not replied Ethel and all the same it is very kind of you to ask me and she smiled more nicely at him.

This is agony cried Mr Salteena clutching hold of a table my life will be sour grapes and ashes without you.

Be a man said Ethel in a gentle whisper and I shall always think of you in a warm manner.

Well half a loaf is better than no bread responded Mr Salteena in a gloomy voice and just then the earl reappeard with a very brisk lady in a tight silk dress whose name was called Lady Gay Finchling and her husband was a General but had been dead a few years. So this is Miss Montacue she began in a rarther high voice. Oh yes said Ethel and Mr Salteena wiped the foaming dew from his forehead. Little did Lady Gay Finchling guess she had just disturbed a proposal of marriage.

The Earl chimed into the conversation now and again and

Lady Gay Finchling told several rather witty stories to enliven the party. Then Bernard Clarke came up and said they had better be going.

Well goodbye Clincham he said I must say I have enjoyed this party most rechauffie I call it dont you Ethel.

Most cried Ethel I suppose you often come she added in a tone of envy to Lady Gay Finchling.

Pretty often said Lady G. F. well goodbye as I see you are in a hurry to be off and she dashed off towards the refreshment place.

Goodbye Ethel said poor Mr Salteena in a spasam and he seized hold of her hand you will one day rue your wicked words farewell he repeated emphatically.

Oh well goodbye said Ethel in a vage tone and then turning to the earl she said I have enjoyed myself very much thankyou.

Please dont mention it cried the earl well goodbye Bernard he added I shall look you up some day at your hotel.

Yes do muttered Bernard always welcome Clincham old boy he added placing his blue crickit cap on his head and so saying he and Ethel left the gay scene and once more oozed forth into the streets of London.

Chapter Nine
A PROPOSALE

NEXT MORNING while imbibing his morning tea beneath his pink silken quilt Bernard decided he must marry Ethel with no more delay. I love the girl he said to himself and she must be mine but I somehow feel I can not propose in London it would not be seemly in the city of London. We must go for a day in the country and when surrounded by the gay twittering of the birds and the smell of the cows I will lay my suit at her feet and he waved his arm wildly at the gay thought. Then he sprang from bed and gave a rat tat at Ethel's door.

Are you up my dear he called.

Well not quite said Ethel hastilly jumping from her downy nest.

Be quick cried Bernard I have a plan to spend a day near Windsor Castle we will take our lunch and spend a happy day.

Oh Hurrah shouted Ethel I shall soon be ready as I had my bath last night so wont wash very much now.

No dont said Bernard and added in a rarther fervent tone through the chink of the door you are fresher than the rose my dear no soap could make you fairer.

Then he dashed off very embarrased to dress. Ethel blushed and felt a bit excited as she heard the words and she put on a new white muslin dress in a fit of high spirits. She looked very beautifull with some red roses in her hat and the dainty red ruge on her cheeks looked quite the thing. Bernard heaved a sigh and his eyes flashed as he beheld her and Ethel thorght to herself what a fine type of manhood he reprisented with his nice thin legs in pale broun trousers and well fitting spats and red rose in his button hole and rarther a sporting cap which gave him a great air with its quaint check and little flaps to pull doun if necesarry. Off they started the envy of all the waiters.

They arrived at Windsor very hot from the jorney and Bernard at once hired a boat to row his beloved up the river. Ethel could not row but she much enjoyed seeing the tough sunburnt arms of Bernard tugging at the oars as she lay among the rich cushons of the dainty boat. She had a rarther lazy nature but Bernard did not know of this. However he soon got dog tired and suggested lunch by the mossy bank.

Oh yes said Ethel quickly opening the sparkling champaigne.

Dont spill any cried Bernard as he carved some chicken.

They eat and drank deeply of the charming viands ending up with merangs and choclates.

Let us now bask under the spreading trees said Bernard in a passionate tone.

Oh yes lets said Ethel and she opened her dainty parasole and sank down upon the long green grass. She closed her eyes but she was far from asleep. Bernard sat beside her in profound silence

51

gazing at her pink face and long wavy eye lashes. He puffed at his pipe for some moments while the larks gaily caroled in the blue sky. Then he edged a trifle closer to Ethels form.

Ethel he murmered in a trembly voice.

Oh what is it said Ethel hastily sitting up.

Words fail me ejaculated Bernard horsly my passion for you is intense he added fervently. It has grown day and night since I first beheld you.

Oh said Ethel in supprise I am not prepared for this and she lent back against the trunk of the tree.

Bernard placed one arm tightly round her. When will you marry me Ethel he uttered you must be my wife it has come to that I love you so intensly that if you say no I shall perforce dash my body to the brink of yon muddy river he panted wildly.

Oh dont do that implored Ethel breathing rarther hard.

Then say you love me he cried.

Oh Bernard she sighed fervently I certinly love you madly you are to me like a Heathen god she cried looking at his manly form and handsome flashing face I will indeed marry you.

How soon gasped Bernard gazing at her intensly.

As soon as possible said Ethel gently closing her eyes.

My Darling whispered Bernard and he seiezed her in his arms we will be marrid next week.

Oh Bernard muttered Ethel this is so sudden.

No no cried Bernard and taking the bull by both horns he kissed her violently on her dainty face. My bride to be he murmered several times.

Ethel trembled with joy as she heard the mistick words.

Oh Bernard she said little did I ever dream of such as this and she suddenly fainted into his out stretched arms.

Oh I say gasped Bernard and laying the dainty burden on the grass he dashed to the waters edge and got a cup full of the fragrant river to pour on his true loves pallid brow.

She soon came to and looked up with a sickly smile take me back to the Gaiety hotel she whispered faintly.

With plesure my darling said Bernard I will just pack up our viands ere I unloose the boat.

Ethel felt better after a few drops of champagne and began to tidy her hair while Bernard packed the remains of the food. Then arm in arm they tottered to the boat.

I trust you have not got an illness my darling murmered Bernard as he helped her in.

Oh no I am very strong said Ethel I fainted from joy she added to explain matters.

Oh I see said Bernard handing her a cushon well some people do he added kindly and so saying they rowed down the dark stream now flowing silently beneath a golden moon. All was silent as the lovers glided home with a joy in their hearts and radiunce on their faces only the sound of the mystearious water lapping against the frail vessle broke the monotony of the night.

So I will end my chapter.

Chapter Ten

PREPARING FOR THE FRAY

THE NEXT few days were indeed bussy for Ethel and Bernard. First of all Ethel got some dainty pink note paper with silver crest on it and sent out invitations in the following terms to all their frends.

Miss Ethel Monticue will be married to Mr Bernard Clarke at Westminster Abbey on June 10th. Your company is requested there at 2-30 sharp and afterwards for refreshment at the Gaiety Hotel.   R.S.V.P.

Having posted heaps of these and got several replies Ethel began to order her wedding dress which cost a good bit. She chose a rich satin with a humped pattern of gold on the pure white and it had a long train edged with Airum lilies. Her veil was of pure lace with a crown of orange blossom. Her bouquett she ordered to be of white dog daisies St. Joseph lilies and orange blossoms tied up with pale blue satin ribbon.

You will indeed be a charming spectacle my darling gasped Bernard as they left the shop. Then they drove to the tailor where Bernard ordered an elligant black suit with coat tails lined with a crimson satin and a pale lavender tie and an opera hat of the same hue and he intended to wear violets in his button holes – also his best white spats diamond studs and a few extras of costly air. They both ordered a lot of new clothes besides and Bernard gave Ethel a very huge tara made of rubies and diamonds also two rich braclets and Ethel gave him a bran new trunk of shiny green leather. The earl of Clincham sent a charming gift of some hem stitched sheets edged with real lace and a photo of himself in a striking attitude. Mr Salteena sent Ethel a bible with a few pious words of advice and regret and he sent Bernard a very handy little camp stool. Ethels parents were too poor to come so far but her mother sent her a gold watch which did not go but had been some years in the family and her father provided a cheque for £2 and promised to send her a darling little baby calf when ready. Then they ordered

the most splendid refreshments they had tea and coffee and sparkling wines to drink also a lovly wedding cake of great height with
a sugar angel at the top holding a sword made of almond paste.

They had countless cakes besides also ices jelly merangs jam
tarts with plenty of jam on each some cold tongue some ham
with salid and a pigs head done up in a wondrous manner. Ethel
could hardly contain herself as she gazed at the sumpshious repast and Bernard gave her a glass of rich wine while he imbibed
some whisky before going to bed. Ethel got speedilly into her bed
for the last time at the dear old Gaiety and shed a few salt tears
thinking of her past life but she quickly cheerd up and began to
plan about how many children she would have. I hope I shall have
a good lot she thought to herself and so saying fell into repose.

Chapter Eleven

THE WEDDING

THE ABBEY was indeed thronged next day when Ethel and Bernard cantered up in a very fine carrage drawn by two prancing steeds who foamed a good deal. In the porch stood several clean altar boys who conducted the lucky pair up the aile while the organ pealed a merry blast. The mighty edifice was packed and seated in the front row was the Earl of Clincham looking very brisk as he was going to give Ethel away at the correct moment. Beside him sat Mr Salteena all in black and looking bitterly sad and he ground his teeth as Ethel came marching up. There were some merry hymns and as soon as Ethel and Bernard were one the clergyman began a sermon about Adam and Eve and the serpent and Mr Salteena cried into his large handkerchief and the earl kept on nudging him as his sniffs were rarther loud. Then the wedding march pealed fourth and doun the church stepped Ethel and Bernard as husband and wife. Into the cab they got and speedelly dashed off to the Gaiety. The wedding refreshments were indeed a treat to all and even Mr Salteena cheered up when he beheld the wedding cake and sparkling wines. Then the earl got up and made a fine speech about marrage vows and bliss and he quoted several good bits from the bible which got a lot of applause. Bernard replied in good round terms. I thank your lordship for those kind remarks he said in clear tones I expect we shall be as happy as a lark and I hope you will all be ditto some day. Here Here muttered a stray lady in the crowd and down sat Bernard while Ethel went up to change her wedding garment for a choice pink velvit dress with a golden gurdle and a very chick toque. Bernard also put on a new suit of blue stripe and some silk socks and clean under clothing. Hurah hurah shouted the guests as the pair reappeard in the aforesaid get ups. Then everybody got a bag of rice and sprinkled on the pair and Mr Salteena sadly threw a white tennis shoe at them wiping his eyes the while. Off drove the happy pair and the guests finished up the food. The happy pair went to Egypt for their Honymoon as they thought it would be a nice warm spot and they had never seen the wondrous land. Ethel was a bit sick on the boat but Bernard braved the storm in manly style. However Ethel had recovered by the time they got to Egypt and here we shall leave them for a merry six weeks of bliss while we return to England.

Chapter Twelve

HOW IT ENDED

Mr Salteena by the aid of the earl and the kindness of the Prince of Wales managed to get the job his soul craved and any day might be seen in Hyde park or Pickadilly galloping madly after the Royal Carrage in a smart suit of green velvit with knickerbockers compleat. At first he was rarther terrified as he was not used to riding and he found his horse bumped him a good deal and he had to cling on desperatly to its flowing main. At other times the horse would stop dead and Mr Salteena would use his spurs and bad languige with no avail. But he soon got more used to his fresh and sultry steed and His Royal Highness seemed satisfide.

The earl continued his merry life at the compartments till finally he fell in love with one of the noble ladies who haunted them. She was not so pretty as Ethel as she had rather a bulgy figure and brown eyes but she had lovly raven tresses a pointed nose and a rose like complexion of a dainty hue. She had very nice feet and plenty of money. Her name was called Lady Helena Herring and her age was 25 and she mated well with the earl.

Mr Salteena grew very lonely after the earl was marrid and he could not bear a single life any more so failing Ethel he married one of the maids in waiting at Buckingham palace by name Bessie Topp a plesant girl of 18 with a round red face and rarther stary eyes.

So now that all our friends are marrid I will add a few words about their familys. Ethel and Bernard returned from their Honymoon with a son and hair a nice fat baby called Ignatius Bernard. They soon had six more children four boys and three girls and some of them were twins which was very exciting.

The earl only got two rarther sickly girls called Helen and Marie because the last one looked slightly french.

Mr Salteena had a large family of 10 five of each but he grew very morose as the years rolled by and his little cottage was very noisy and his wife was a bit annoying at times especially when he took to dreaming of Ethel and wishing he could have marrid her – Still he was a pius man in his way and found relief in prayer.

Bernard Clark was the happiest of our friends as he loved Ethel to the bitter end and so did she him and they had a nice house too.

The earl soon got tired of his sickly daughters and his wife had a savage temper so he thought he would divorce her and try again but he gave up the idear after several attempts and decided to offer it up as a Mortification.

So now my readers we will say farewell to the characters in this book.

The End
by Daisy Ashford

A NOTE ON THE TEXT

For this edition the text has been transcribed from a photocopy
of the original holograph, written in pencil at Lewes, Sussex in
1890 when Daisy Ashford was nine years old. This manuscript,
contained in a red-covered exercise book, is now in the Berg Col-
lection of the New York Public Library.

The text as hitherto published differs in certain respects
from the text of the manuscript. Many new paragraph divisions
were introduced, 'for the reader's comfort' as J. M. Barrie put it,
and some were removed. Some twenty errors in spelling and
punctuation, regarded as inadvertent, were silently amended.
The first letters of some words were capitalized, e.g. the 'e' in the
earl of Clincham. Some spellings were standardized with varying
degrees of justification, e.g. Clark (9 appearances in the manuscript), Clarke (8); Monticue (5), Montacue (6); rarther (8), rather
(24); privite (1), private (5). In each of these cases the former
spelling was invariably used in the printed text. A few further
differences may be ascribed to simple errors in transcription; the

most notable of these was in the title, 'Visiters' being substituted for 'Viseters'. In six cases, only three of which could be considered inadvertent errors, words were introduced or deleted, in one a word was substituted.

The numbers of the chapters were also standardized. The author had given no number to 'The First Evening' (Chapter Three) but had designated both 'High Life' and the subsequent chapter (only given a title – 'Bernards Idear' – when the book was published) as Chapter Six, and both 'A Proposale' and 'Preparing for the Fray' as Chapter Ten.

The effect of these changes was to tidy up the text and to make it easier to follow, but they also had the effect of presenting an erratic speller as a consistently bad one.

The text in this edition aims to reproduce the original in all respects apart from the following. The paragraph divisions added to previous editions have been retained and simple slips of spelling and punctuation, e.g. sreets for streets, including the eccentric chapter numbering, have been corrected. More controversially, it has also been decided to retain the spelling 'Visiters' in the title, although 'Viseters' is the manuscript spelling. In a few cases the intended spelling is not clear and there the form most frequently used by the author has been preferred.